Ben's Story

By Pamela Rushby

Illustrated by Tom Jellett

Chapter 1

A Problem

When I started at this new school, I knew they'd find out about me. I didn't expect it'd be on the very first day, but it was.

The teacher, Mr. Lee, introduced me. "This is Ben," he said. "I know you'll make him feel welcome."

"Hi, Ben," everyone said cheerfully.

"Hi," I mumbled. I didn't expect to be here long enough to make friends.

"Now, where shall we put you?" Mr. Lee said. "Ah, next to Jon, I think. You'll look after Ben, won't you, Jon?"

The kid called Jon said, "Sure," and grinned, but I didn't smile back.

I sat down and looked around the room. It didn't look much different than all the other classrooms I'd been in, and I'd been in a lot of classrooms.

My family moves around a lot, so I've been to ten different schools, and I'm only nine. Maybe that was the reason I had a problem – a big problem.

Chapter 2

What I Did on My Vacation

Mr. Lee took attendance. Then he handed out paper and pencils and wrote something on the whiteboard. "There you go," he said. "Two pages from each of you, please, before lunch."

The class groaned. "Not 'What I Did on My Vacation,' Mr. Lee!" they protested. "Not again!"

Mr. Lee grinned. "At least you'll all have something to write about," he said. "You all did *something* during the summer!"

The class groaned again, but they all started working. I picked up my pencil and tried to look as if I was thinking.

Beside me that Jon kid was writing away. I couldn't believe it – he'd filled half a page already.

Mr. Lee walked around the room. He stopped beside me and said, "Not started yet, Ben?"

"No," I said.

"So what did you do during the summer?" Mr. Lee asked.

"Nothing much," I said. "Well, I went on five trips with my dad."

"*Five trips?*" said Mr. Lee. "That's a lot of traveling."

"My dad drives trucks," I said. "I go along with him for company."

"You could write about that, couldn't you?" said Mr. Lee.

"Yeah," I said. "I guess I could."

"Get started then," said Mr. Lee, and he walked away.

I could see that Jon kid looking at me, and I could also see he'd written a whole page.

"Show off!" I thought.

Chapter 3

Big Things

Mr. Lee walked by again and said, "Still no inspiration, Ben?"

I shook my head.

"Tell me about the things you see on the road," Mr. Lee said. "What do you like best?"

That was easy! "I like the big things," I said.

"Big things?" said Mr. Lee.

"Yes," I said. "There's a Big Banana and a Big Shrimp and a Big Cow and a Big Pineapple. They're cool." I told Mr. Lee all about them – how you could go inside the Big Cow and climb all the way to the top of the Big Pineapple.

"Great!" said Mr. Lee. "Write about big things, then!"

8

I started to write. I wrote two lines. Then I looked at them and erased some words. I turned my back to stop that Jon kid from looking at my writing. He was up to three pages.

When Mr. Lee came back, I'd still only written two lines, and I could tell he was getting annoyed with me. "Better get busy, Ben," he said. "If the big things are no good, write about the places you like best. What are they?"

"I like one place where there are hills covered with sugarcane," I said. "The sugarcane runs right down to the sea. The wind blows through the sugarcane, making it move like waves in a sea. Only it's a green sea, not a blue one."

"Yes?" said Mr. Lee.

"And I like the rain forest," I said. "It's all cool and dim and musty smelling, and the trees stretch up so high you can't see the sky."

"Excellent!" said Mr. Lee. "Beautiful words! Write them down, Ben."

But I didn't. I just sat, and that Jon kid kept writing and writing and writing – making me look bad!

I thought, "I'll get you at lunchtime!"

Chapter 4

Ben's Story

"Time to finish up," Mr. Lee called out. "There's just time to read a few stories out loud before lunch. Do I have any volunteers?" He stopped by me and looked at the two messy, rubbed-out lines I'd written.

"Hmmm," he said. "There's a problem, isn't there, Ben?" I didn't say anything. "You've got a problem with writing," he said quietly. "That's nothing to be worried about. We can fix it. What about your reading – how's that?"

"Not too good," I mumbled.

"We can fix that, too," Mr. Lee said, "just as long as we know. It'll be OK. I'll talk to you later."

I just knew that Jon kid had heard every word. He knew I couldn't read or write properly! I was *really* going to get him at lunchtime!

"Who'd like to read their stories out loud?" Mr. Lee asked.

A few kids put up their hands, but Jon's was up first. "Can I read Ben's story, Mr. Lee?" he called out.

I stared at him. What did he mean, my story? There was no "my story" – well, only two lines of it. Was that Jon kid making fun of me?

"Show me what you mean, Jon," said Mr. Lee.

Jon showed Mr. Lee what he'd been writing. There were five pages at least. Mr. Lee looked carefully at it. Then he smiled and said, "Go ahead, Jon."

I slid down in my chair. That Jon kid was in *big* trouble at lunchtime!

Then Jon started to speak. "I wrote Ben's story down," he said, "just the way he told it because it was really good." He cleared his throat. "Ben's Story," he read. "I like the Big Things – they're cool! You can go right inside the Big Cow. You can climb right to the top of the Big Pineapple . . . "

He kept reading – about the way the sugarcane fields look like a green sea and the way the rain forest is cool and dim and so thick you can't see the sky. When he'd finished, everyone was quiet.

"Beautiful words," said Mr. Lee at last. "I think that should be printed in the school newsletter. You're a real writer, Ben!"

"A writer?" I said. "But . . . but I can't . . . I mean . . . "

"Oh, *that!*" said Mr. Lee. "We'll soon fix that! Class – a round of applause for Ben's story!"

Chapter 5

Maybe . . .

Everyone clapped and smiled, and this time, I smiled back. When Jon sat down beside me, I smiled at him, too.

Maybe I was going to like this school. Maybe this time I'd make some friends. Maybe soon I wouldn't have a problem.

Lots of maybes, I thought, but one thing was for sure. I wasn't going to get Jon at lunchtime!